USBORNE FIRST READING
Old Mother Hubbard
Retold by Russell Punter
Illustrated by Fred Blunt

USBORNE FIRST READING
The Genie in the Bottle
Retold by Rosie Dickins
Illustrated by Sara Rojo

USBORNE FIRST READING
Stone Soup
Retold by Lesley Sims
Illustrated by Georgien Overwater

USBORNE FIRST READING
The Baobab Tree
Retold by Louie Stowell
Illustrated by Laure Fournier

USBORNE FIRST READING
The Old Woman who lived in a Shoe
Retold by Russell Punter
Illustrated by Joelle Dreidemy

USBORNE YOUNG READING
The Little Giraffe
Retold by Lesley Sims
Illustrated by Laure Fournier

USBORNE FIRST READING
The Roly-Poly Rice Ball
Retold by Rosie Dickins
Illustrated by Ben Mantle

USBORNE FIRST READING
Brer Rabbit and the Blackberry Bush
Retold by Louie Stowell
Illustrated by

USBORNE FIRST READING
How Bear Lost his Tail

Doctor Foster went to Gloucester

Retold by Russell Punter

Illustrated by David Semple

Reading consultant: Alison Kelly
Roehampton University

Doctor Foster went
to Gloucester,

in a shower of rain.

He stepped in a puddle,

right up to his middle,

and never went there again.

Doctor Foster went
to Oxford,

in a cloud of fog.

He just couldn't see,

bumped into a tree

and splat! He fell
into a bog.

Doctor Foster went
to Gosport,

in a howling gale.

The wind was so strong,

it blew him along,

and he flew down the
street with a wail.

Doctor Foster went
to Stockton,

in the swirling snow.

The frost bit his nose,

his spectacles froze

and he couldn't see
which way to go.

Doctor Foster went to Bognor,

in the sizzling heat.

He took off his socks,

fell asleep on
some rocks

and got sunburned all over his feet.

Doctor Foster
told his daughter,

"I'm not going to roam."

"I'll see patients here,

with my family near."

"From now on, there's
no place like home."

PUZZLES

Puzzle 1

Can you spot the differences between these two pictures? There are six to find.

Puzzle 2

Match the weather to the picture.

wind fog rain snow

1.

2.

3.

4.

Puzzle 3

Find these things in the picture.

cat hat bird bag

puddle cloud

Answers to puzzles

Puzzle 1

Puzzle 2

1. 

snow

2. 

rain

3. 

wind

4. 

fog

Puzzle 3

About the rhyme

The original version of *Doctor Foster* appeared in 1810. The rhyme we know today was first published in 1844. Some people think it is about Edward I of England (1239-1307). There is a story that, on a visit to Gloucester, he fell off his horse into a puddle and swore he would never return.

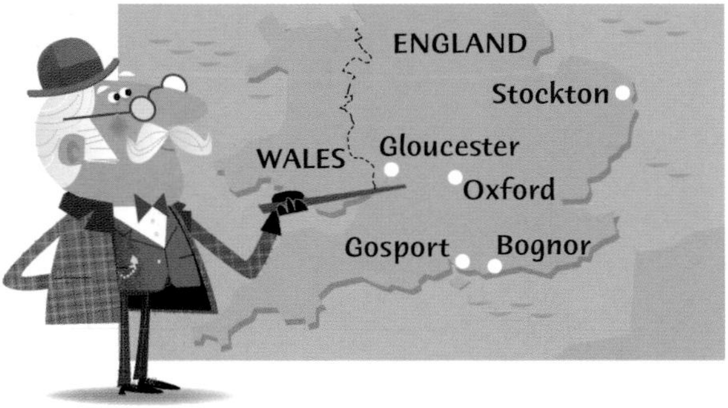

Series editor: Lesley Sims

First published in 2012 by Usborne Publishing Ltd., Usborne House, 83-85 Saffron Hill, London EC1N 8RT, England. www.usborne.com

UE. First published in America in 2012.

USBORNE FIRST READING
Level Three

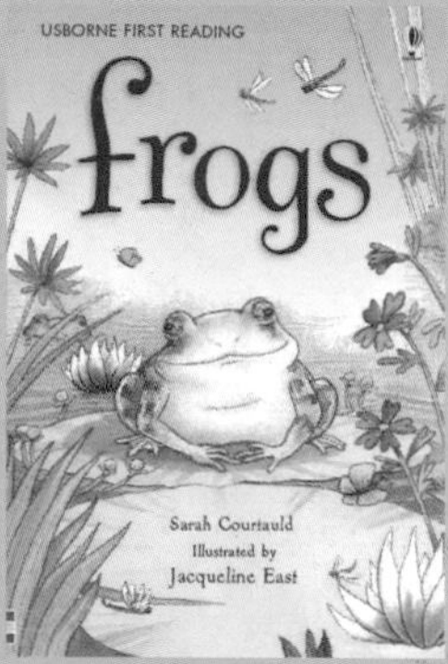

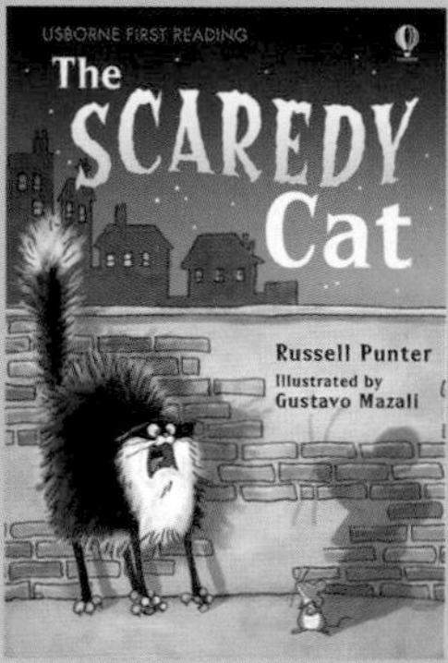